DOES A MOUSE HAVE A MOMMY?

Fred Ehrlich, M.D.
Pictures by Emily Bolam

🍎 Blue Apple Books
Maplewood, N.J.

For mommies everywhere

Text copyright © 2004 by Fred Ehrlich
Illustrations copyright © 2004 by Emily Bolam
All rights reserved
CIP Data is available.
First published in the United States 2004 by
🍎 Blue Apple Books
P.O. Box 1380, Maplewood, N.J. 07040
www.blueapplebooks.com
First published in paperback by Blue Apple Books 2007
Distributed in the U.S. by Chronicle Books

First Paperback Edition
Printed in China

ISBN 13: 978-1-59354-589-5
ISBN 10: 1-59354-589-4

1 3 5 7 9 10 8 6 4 2

Every animal baby has a mother and a father.
Female turtles and lizards lay eggs.

Turtle babies, called hatchlings, are able to crawl
away and find food as soon as they are born.
They are not taken care of by their parents.

Lizards are also on their own when they are born.
A baby lizard hatches along with twenty others.

A lizard baby never knows which big lizard is
its father and which one is its mother.

Does a spider have a mommy?
A spider mother carries her eggs in a silken case and protects them. She can carry as many as 200 eggs. Once the eggs hatch, the spiderlings are on their own.

Does a mouse have a mommy?
A baby mouse is taken care of by its mother,
but not by its father.

Baby mice are born blind, deaf, and without fur.
Babies drink mother's milk for about a week,
then they find their own food. A mouse
grows to full size in less than two months.
Then it can have babies of its own.

Some animal mothers work very hard
to take care of their babies.
A baby camel drinks a gallon of its mother's
milk every day for a whole year.

Camels travel in herds, which are led by the oldest females. A camel mother protects her own baby within the herd.

Baby kangaroos, or joeys, are also taken care of by their mothers and not by their fathers.

The mother carries the baby in her pouch for a long time... more than six months. Because a kangaroo baby is very small and helpless at birth, it stays in the pouch and nurses on its mother's milk.

After a while, it can climb out of the pouch
and hop around, then climb in again.

Polar bears live where it's cold. During the winter, while the bear mother is in her den, she gives birth to one to three cubs.

The cubs are born hairless and blind, but the body heat of the mother keeps them warm, and her milk keeps them well fed.

When spring comes and the babies are bigger, they get their first look at the outside world.

The babies stay with their mother for two years, learning how to hunt for food for themselves.

Elephants are very big, and so are elephant babies.
Each baby weighs more than 200 pounds!

A mother elephant gives birth to one baby.
The baby, or calf, stays with its mother for at
least three years and sometimes more.

Elephants travel in herds made up of females and young males. Adult males, including the fathers of the babies, travel alone.

Everyone in the herd helps protect the babies.

Monkeys are primates, the group of animals that includes baboons, apes, and people.

When primate babies are born, they can't do anything for themselves.

This monkey mommy baby-sits while the daddy looks for food. She carries the baby and protects it from enemies.

Monkeys, baboons, and apes all spend a long time with their parents—two to three years—before they leave the group and venture out on their own.

But no animal spends as long in its parents' care as a child.

A human has the longest childhood of any animal.

Human parents spend more time—sixteen or more years—taking care of children than any other animal parents.

They carry them, play with them,
feed them, dress them,
and protect them.

Mothers and fathers help them learn:

To talk

To keep themselves clean

To stay safe

To follow rules

To get along with others

To read and write

Mommies are special.
Isn't yours?